Sejal Sinha
Dives for Diamonds
on Neptune

Also by Maya Prasad:

Sejal Sinha Battles Superstorms
Sejal Sinha Swims with Sea Dragons

Sejal Sinha

Dives for Diamonds on Neptune

BY MAYA PRASAD ★ ILLUSTRATED BY ABIRA DAS

ALADDIN

New York London Toronto Sydney New Delhi

This book is a work of fiction. Any references to historical events, real people, or real places are used fictitiously. Other names, characters, places, and events are products of the author's imagination, and any resemblance to actual events or places or persons, living or dead, is entirely coincidental.

ALADDIN

An imprint of Simon & Schuster Children's Publishing Division
1230 Avenue of the Americas, New York, New York 10020
First Aladdin paperback edition January 2024
Text copyright © 2024 by Maya Prasad
Illustrations copyright © 2024 by Abira Das
Also available in an Aladdin hardcover edition.
All rights reserved, including the right of reproduction in whole or in part in any form.
ALADDIN and related logo are registered trademarks of Simon & Schuster, Inc.
Simon & Schuster: Celebrating 100 Years of Publishing Since 1924
For information about special discounts for bulk purchases, please contact
Simon & Schuster Special Sales at 1-866-506-1949 or business@simonandschuster.com.
The Simon & Schuster Speakers Bureau can bring authors to your live event. For
more information or to book an event contact the Simon & Schuster Speakers Bureau
at 1-866-248-3049 or visit our website at www.simonspeakers.com.
Designed by Heather Palisi
The illustrations for this book were rendered digitally.
The text of this book was set in Berling Nova Text Pro.
Manufactured in the United States of America 1123 OFF
2 4 6 8 10 9 7 5 3 1
CIP data for this book is available from the Library of Congress.
ISBN 9781665911849 (hc)
ISBN 9781665911832 (pbk)
ISBN 9781665911856 (ebook)

For Mom & Dad:
thanks for always nurturing my curiosity and my big
dreams!

—M. P.
To those rare, beautiful friendships that shine bright
like diamonds! You inspire me every day.
—A. D.

 CONTENTS

Sejal Sinha

Dives for Diamonds on Neptune

CHAPTER ONE
The "Monster" in Fluff Monster

Give that back!" I yelled. "I need it!"

My cookies-and-cream colored pup, Fluff Monster, had my precious purple notebook between her teeth.

It was a really important notebook, the one I used for brainstorming possible next adventures. I wrote down all my ideas in there, whether they were good or bad.

As I lunged for the notebook, Fluff Monster scurried away. She was a small dog, but even with such short legs, she could dart out of reach pretty quickly. She hopped up into the cardboard box that could turn into whatever I wanted it to: a submarine, an airplane, even a spaceship. Maybe she was ready for a new mission. After all, I'd taken her to lots of cool places already. We'd flown into a hurricane. We'd gone to hydrothermal vents at the bottom of the sea. I just didn't know what to do next.

"Do you have any ideas for a new adventure?" I asked Fluff.

But instead of answering, she hopped right out the other side, and then dashed up the basement stairs.

"Fluff Monster!" I shouted, rushing after her.

She'd been so naughty lately. Even though I loved her like a little sister, I was getting kind of tired of it. Maybe I should leave her behind on my next mission. Then I could focus on the things I cared about, like adventure and glory and all that. Instead of making sure she wasn't chewing on things she wasn't supposed to chew on.

Fluff ran past the kitchen, where my five-year-old brother, Abu, was on the kitchen floor, screaming and banging his fists on the tiles.

"What's the matter with him?" I asked.

Dad rubbed his eyes. "He finished his string cheese."

"I thought we had a mountain of them in the pantry!"

"We do." Dad sighed. "He's just mad that the one in his hand somehow disappeared. You know, because he ate it."

Oh boy. Fluff had been naughty lately, but Abu kept having a fit over anything and everything. But I didn't have time to help Dad with Abu right now because I needed to get that notebook.

I heard Fluff padding across the dining room and sprinted after her. My grandparents were reading magazines and drinking chai at the table. They still looked very sleepy even though it was almost lunchtime. They had come back to the US late last night—all the way from India. They'd been visiting there for a whole month.

"Where are you off to?" Nana said with a yawn.

"Fluff Monster stole my notebook!" I said, running past him.

"Bribe her with a treat," Nani suggested.

Actually, that wasn't a bad idea. I went back into the kitchen and grabbed one of her favorite peanut butter biscuits. Then I followed the sound of her paws scampering across the hallway, into the den. Mom and my twelve-year-old cousin Ash were sitting at the messy desk, looking at Ash's science fair report on a laptop.

"Wow, so it really rains diamonds on Neptune?" Ash asked.

What? Diamond rain? For real? That distracted me from Fluff and the notebook.

CHAPTER TWO
Idea Muncher

When we recreated the conditions on Neptune in our lab, " Mom said, "tiny diamonds did form. But it's only theoretical at this point."

Mom was an astrophysicist. That meant she studied stars and outer-space stuff. She worked in a lab and did experiments, and had to give lots of talks with fancy slides to impress people so she could do even more experiments. I usually didn't pay too much attention, but diamond rain sounded pretty cool.

"So you don't know for sure?" Ash returned.

"Nope. I'm sure you've read that no spacecraft has made it into Neptune's interior . . ."

The sound of pages being torn reminded me of my naughty puppy. I bent down to find Fluff Monster munching on a page out of my notebook, which was lying next to her. Covered in puppy drool. Yuck.

I grabbed it and flipped the pages to find what was missing. "No, no, no . . ."

"Are you okay, honey?" Mom asked, putting a hand on my back.

"No!" I yelled. "Fluff Monster ate all my ideas!"

"I'm sorry, dear," Mom said. "I hope you can remember them."

I sniffled. "I don't know."

"Why don't you take Fluff Monster for a walk?" Mom said. "She probably took your notebook because she was bored and wanted attention."

"She doesn't deserve a walk!" I wailed.

"If she gets more exercise, she'll be too tired to get into trouble," Mom said. "Besides, you promised that you would help out if we got a puppy. I expect you to keep that promise."

"I'll come with you," Ash offered. "I could use a break from my homework."

Mom ruffled their hair. "You've been working hard. A break sounds good. You can finish up your report later."

"Okay, Mausi." Ash smiled.

They were one of my coolest cousins. They had electric-blue hair and matching wing-shaped glasses and always wore lots of funky clothes. Today they wore a green blazer with a sparkly tie and black jeans with stars patched all over them. I always wished I could be more like Ash, but Mom would never let me dye my hair. Also, being twelve sounded hard. Ash always had so much homework. I felt like I already had enough chores to do right now, and I was only eight.

I sighed. "Let's get this walk over with, then."

Ash patted my back. "That's the spirit!"

CHAPTER THREE
The Snot Disaster

Of course Dad made us take Abu on the walk too. Probably because he was tired of Abu's string cheese tantrum. Fluff and Abu were driving everyone up the wall!

It was nice to get outside, though. The sun shone brightly, and spring flowers were growing everywhere.

"Achoo!" Ash's sneeze was loud enough to startle Fluff.

"Allergies?" I asked.

"Spring isn't my favorite," Ash said. "But at least Fluff likes it."

Fluff sniffed a bush full of flowers, her tail wagging happily.

Abu tugged on my sleeve. "Can I hold the leash?"

"No!" I kept a tight hold of it. "You'll probably drop it, and then we'll have to chase her all over the neighborhood."

"That only happened once!"

"It happened three times last week."

"You're bossy!" Abu glared angrily at me.

"Am not," I said.

"Well," Ash said, "maybe you could give Abu another chan—achoo! Achoo!"

"Are you okay?" I asked.

Ash blew their nose into a tissue. "Achoo! Um, I'm fine. Anyway, Abu won't learn unless you give him a chance."

"No, he'll get us in trouble," I insisted. "I don't want to have to chase after Fluff when he lets go of the leash again."

10

Abu stomped his feet. "You're the meanest!"

I ignored him, and we kept walking in silence. Well not exactly silence, since Ash sneezed about a million more times.

At the dog park, Fluff Monster got excited and started tugging hard on the leash. She wheezed in her harness while bounding toward her best friend in the world, a little terrier named Bandit.

"Hi!" Amy, Bandit's owner, waved at us. "Those two just can't stay apart!"

"Does Fluff somehow know when Bandit's going to be here?" I freed Fluff from the leash since the park was fenced in.

"She must have good instincts," Ash said. "Achoo!"

Fluff sprinted to sniff Bandit. After saying their doggie hellos, they began running in circles together, playing puppy tag.

"Achoo!" This time Ash sneezed so hard that snot was hanging out of their nose in a long slimy ribbon. "Shoot. I'm out of tissues."

I didn't have any, but Amy dug around in her

purse and found a pack. As she handed one to Ash, a kid with floppy brown hair and a big smile came up.

"Ash? What're you doing here?"

"Ack!" My cousin fumbled with the tissue, turning around to blow hard. Finally, they faced us—with a big silly grin on their face.

"Um, hi. I'm hanging with my cousins." Ash gestured at me and Abu. "Sejal, Abu, this is Leo. He goes to my school."

Leo waved at us. "Cool. My parents and I come here sometimes because this is Finster's favorite dog park. Here he is now."

Finster was missing a tail and an eye but didn't seem very bothered by it. He was so friendly and sat down in front of me. Fluff never sat down for strangers like that!

"He's adorable!" Ash commented, then started sneezing again.

"You okay?" Leo asked.

"Totally fine. Spring allergies. Um, have you started your science fair project?"

Leo nodded. "I swiped some bacteria off the door handles from a bunch of public places, and now they're blooming in my petri dishes."

"That sounds gross."

"Yeah, exactly." Leo suddenly started laughing. "By the way . . . you've got a . . . booger."

Ash yelped and wiped at their nose frantically. But then another sneezing fit hit them, and it was a waterfall of snot.

"Hey, could I get a swab of that for my project?" Leo joked.

But Ash was already running out of the park.

CHAPTER FOUR
Tears and Tantrums

I couldn't believe Ash had run off without us. As Abu and I walked home, my little brother tugged on my sleeve again. "Can I hold the leash now? Fluff is too tired to chase any squirrels or run away."

"Sometimes she gets extra naughty when she's tired," I said. "So I think I better keep the leash."

Abu stomped his feet and let out a big scream. Uh-oh.

"We're almost home, anyway," I said, hoping he wasn't about to have a total meltdown, like he'd had in the kitchen with Dad earlier. Maybe he was hungry. "You can have another string cheese pack then!"

But he wasn't in the mood to listen. He collapsed onto the sidewalk and started beating his fists and kicking his legs.

"You're too old for this," I said.

But he just kept screaming and beating his fists. Meanwhile, Fluff had spotted a squirrel and was pulling on the leash to chase after it. I wanted to leave them both behind—but then I'd really get in trouble.

I wished I could escape on one of my adventures, take a rocket ship straight out of here. I closed my eyes, imagining I was blasting off. Maybe to Neptune? With that diamond rain that Ash and Mom had been talking about?

Eventually, Abu got tired of his tantrum. Maybe because he noticed I wasn't even watching him anymore. With a huff, he got up and started marching home. Fluff seemed to sense the mood and stopped tugging on the leash.

We found Ash sitting on the steps of the front porch. To my surprise, they were crying.

"Okay, Abu." I handed the leash to him. "You can take Fluff in from here."

Even though it was only a few feet to our front door, he looked very proud of himself. He and Fluff dashed inside. I picked up a fallen empty string cheese wrapper from the front walk and then sat down beside Ash.

"What's the matter?" I asked.

"That was humiliating!" Ash sobbed harder.

"I don't think Leo minded about the snot," I said. "I mean, he just wanted a sample for his science project."

Ash shook their head. "Yeah, right. Now he'll always think of me as Snot-Covered Kid, don't you think? And what if he tells his friends at school about it?"

I hadn't thought about that. Leo seemed nice, but sometimes kids did tell embarrassing stories like that.

Ash stood up. "I wish I could fly to Neptune and never come back. Achoo!"

Wait, Ash wanted to go to Neptune too? That got me excited. Me and Ash—and nobody else. Definitely not annoying little brothers or naughty puppies. A thrill went through me.

"Let's go, then!" I said, grabbing Ash's hand. It was time for an adventure!

CHAPTER FIVE
Lehengas, Pashmina Shawls, and More Beautiful Things

Just then, Nani leaned her head out the door. "AASHHH! SAY-JULL!! Come inside! Nana and I have some gifts for you two."

Gifts? Even though I was anxious to get going to Neptune, Nani and Nana did always bring back the best presents from India, including the marble candlesticks that decorated our dining table and the painting of a dancing woman that hung above our mantel. I couldn't wait to see what they'd brought back this time.

We all gathered in the living room, including my parents and Abu and naughty Fluff. Nani and Nana looked slightly more awake now and were both sitting on the sofa, a pile of gifts between them.

"Ash, this is for you." Nani held out a wooden swan. "This sandalwood carving is from Kerala. I really liked the artist's details."

Ash touched its long, graceful neck. "Very pretty. Thanks, Nani and Nana!"

"Ooh, it smells nice too," I said.

"It really does," Ash said, smiling. Their eyes were still a bit puffy, and they looked tired, but at least they weren't sneezing anymore.

"This one is for you, Sejal." Nani took out a shimmering gold-and-red lehenga. "What do you think?"

I held it up against my body. It looked like it would fit perfectly. "I love it. Thanks, Nani and Nana!"

For Mom, they had a sea-green scarf.

"Ooh, thanks," Mom said. "Sejal, this is called

a pashmina shawl. They weave these in Kashmir. They're so soft—do you want to feel it?"

I touched the fabric. It was as soft as a cloud.

Nani and Nana had brought Dad, Abu, and Ash each a fancy kurta and some more beautiful carved figurines.

"You always bring us the most beautiful things," I said. "I want to give you something too."

"No need," Nani said. "We're happy just to spend time with you."

I knew I didn't *need* to give them something, but I really did want to. After all, they always brought back the best souvenirs from their trips. Plus, I had the perfect idea for something extra special to give them from one of mine!

CHAPTER SIX
Mission: Dive for Diamonds on Neptune

Ash," I said, "Let's get Nani and Nana the best souvenir ever!"

I did a cartwheel across the basement carpet. There wasn't the usual mess of toys all over it, since I'd cleaned up for my grandparents' visit. The only thing I'd left out was my cardboard box, for inspiration. And then Fluff had stolen my notebook and distracted me.

"Like what?" Ash asked, lounging on the basement sofa.

"A diamond! From Neptune!!" I stood on my head, my feet leaning against the wall. "You said you wanted to go there, right?"

Ash shrugged. "Is this one of your cardboard box adventures?"

"Yeah, aren't you excited?"

But Ash just shrugged again.

"Come on! This was your idea in the first place!" I somersaulted and did another cartwheel.

I was feeling extra energetic now that I had an idea for a new mission. "Fluff Monster is taking a nap on Nani's lap, and Abu is playing Go Fish with Nana. It's the perfect time for us to escape. Just the two of us."

Spending the day with Ash sounded so fun. Especially since we'd be treasure hunting! Nani and Nana were going to be so impressed.

"Come on," I said, nudging their shoulder. "Neptune doesn't have any pollen, does it? You'll be safe from snot there."

But Ash stayed slumped on the sofa. They really were in a major funk. Maybe talking science would help. They usually got excited about that.

"If it rains diamonds on Neptune, wouldn't it hurt your head?" I asked.

Ash giggled. Finally! Science had worked!

"Did I hear something about treasure?" Professor Cheetah said, climbing out of the toy bin where she'd been resting.

CHAPTER SEVEN
A Hard Bargain

Professor Cheetah was the smartest and best of all my stuffies. She tended to go all quiet around grown-ups, but she and Ash had always gotten along.

"It rains diamonds on Neptune!" I said.

"Actually," Ash said, "humans have never been on Neptune, so we don't know for sure. But in your mom's laboratory experiment, they made everything as much like Neptune as they could. And tiny diamonds really did form. But on Neptune, they would be much bigger."

"How big?" I asked.

Ash shrugged and spread their arms as wide as they could. "As big as icebergs!"

"Whoa!" I said. "So why hasn't anyone ever gone to hunt treasure there before?"

"Neptune is too far away," Ash said. "The only spacecraft that has gotten close was *Voyager* 2 in 1977. It's all in my science fair report."

"Maybe it's too far away for grown-ups," I said. "But my cardboard box can do it. Come on, Professor Cheetah. Let's make our flight plan."

"It's not going to be easy," Professor Cheetah said. "There's a lot of hard math we have to do in order to chart the course to Neptune."

"What do you mean?" I walked over to my map of the solar system, which was on the basement wall. Eight planets moved in a path around the sun: Mercury, Venus, Earth, Mars, Jupiter, Saturn, Uranus, and finally Neptune. Their paths around the sun were called their orbits. There were also small dwarf planets in our solar system, like Pluto and Eris, but I wasn't counting those. I traced a straight line from Earth to Neptune on the map. "See? It's easy!"

"Wrong." Professor Cheetah flicked her tail. "Every second, all the planets in the solar system are moving around the sun. If you follow a straight line from where Earth is now to where Neptune is now, Neptune won't be there anymore. While you're traveling, it will move farther along its orbit."

I tried to picture what she was telling me. Earth was speeding on its orbit around the sun. The sun was moving in the Milky Way galaxy. I knew from school that billions of other stars and planets in the galaxy were also all moving. Even the galaxy itself was moving. And the universe, which contains all the galaxies, was getting bigger. I felt a little dizzy thinking about it all.

I bit my lip. "That sounds complicated."

"I'm excellent at math and happy to do it," Professor Cheetah said, "but you have to share some of the treasure with me. I want half." She grinned her toothy cheetah grin. It was honestly a little scary, but we're best friends anyway.

"Half!" I didn't think that was fair. "I already have to share the treasure with Ash!"

Professor Cheetah crossed her arms. "You won't find any of Neptune's diamonds without me."

I turned to Ash. "Can you make the flight plan?"

They shook their head. "Sorry, the math is way too complicated for me."

"Face it, you need me." Professor Cheetah's whiskers twitched in a cat laugh.

Ugh. She was such an annoying know-it-all sometimes. But she was also right. We needed her help, or we'd never get to that treasure. Plus, I was in a hurry to get going before Fluff Monster woke up from her nap or Abu came downstairs and decided to throw another tantrum over who knows what.

"Fine, we can divide the treasure into three parts," I finally agreed. "Ash gets one share, I get one share, and you get one share."

"One-third of the treasure?" Professor Cheetah

licked her paws, thinking. "It's a very discounted rate, but I accept."

Thank goodness.

Professor Cheetah drew a new map with lots of math formulas filling up the side. I had no idea what they meant, but having a know-it-all best friend was useful. We were all set to hunt diamonds on Neptune!

CHAPTER EIGHT
Sneaks and Stowaways

We got to work, and it wasn't long before the cardboard box was space-worthy. We'd added thrusters (also known as pillows) and a control panel (made of stickers). Professor Cheetah was in charge of the mechanics.

"Ready to escape?" I asked Ash.

"More than anything." Ash shuddered, probably thinking of Leo and the Snot Disaster. I couldn't wait to get away either. Away from little brothers who threw tantrums. Away from naughty pups who ate my best ideas.

We got in and I started the countdown. "10! 9! 8! 7! 6! 5! 4! 3! 2! 1!"

The room shook. The basement ceiling split wide open, but when I looked up, I didn't see the rest of the house. There was only the big blue sky. The cardboard box got very hot as the rockets fired. It was time to press the most important button: a very special green triangle sticker on the control panel.

Triangles have a lot of strength and power, and this one would help us escape Earth's gravity. It was a button that took the power of your imagination and changed all that energy into something amazing.

I carefully pushed the green triangle button, and presto! The cardboard box expanded into a real rocket ship. We zoomed out toward fluffy white clouds.

I held on tight to my seat. The rocket ship got even hotter as we shot up past the clouds of Earth's atmosphere. And then we were in space.

Surrounded by darkness and stars that twinkled like the diamonds I wanted to find so badly. Earth looked like a giant blue, green, and white marble dangling outside the window.

I floated out of my seat. So did Ash and Professor Cheetah.

"Whee!" Ash said. "This is so cool! I forgot how strong your imagination is, Sejal!"

I beamed. "Thanks!"

"Also," they said, "I should really add something in my report about weightlessness. It happens when you're really far away from a planet's gravity."

"Gravity?" I asked.

"It's the force that brings you back to the ground when you fall or jump," Ash explained. "But when you're in space, gravity from nearby planets is much weaker. You can bounce around however you want! Weightlessness also happens when you're spinning around the Earth, like if you're on a satellite."

With that explanation, Ash did a somersault

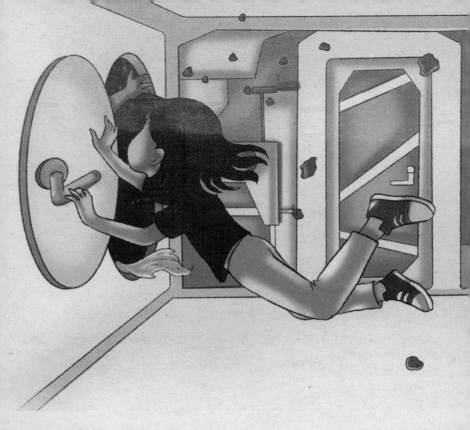

through the air. They looked really happy. Maybe we really had left all our problems behind on Earth.

"Wheeeeeee!" I followed their lead, laughing and doing a midair flip. "Space gymnastics!"

"Let's do this!" Professor Cheetah cartwheeled across the cabin, touching the ceiling and the floor as she went.

"Arf! Arf! Arf!" The sound came from behind a hatch door that had appeared when the cardboard box had changed into a real ship.

"What was that?" I spun the wheel on the hatch to open it.

As soon as I did, little pieces of doggie kibble floated past me. And then so did Fluff Monster—and Abu!

I couldn't believe it. This trip was supposed to be just me and Ash and Professor Cheetah! My escape from big-sister stuff!

Fluff wagged her tail as she floated past me, barking excitedly. Her four little legs spun like she was riding an invisible bike, but she didn't know how to push off a wall to get where she wanted to go. It was pretty cute, but she still wasn't supposed to be here.

Abu somersaulted in the air too. "Wheeeee!"

"How did you get here?" I demanded. "I thought you were playing Go Fish and that Fluff was napping."

"We snuck on!" Abu sounded proud of himself. "You can't just leave us behind!"

I wanted to stomp my feet and throw a tantrum just the like the one Abu had when I wouldn't give him the leash. But it was hard to stomp when you were weightless.

Ash floated over to pet Fluff. "You have to admit, she's a cute stowaway."

Traitor.

A piece of floating kibble bumped Abu in the forehead, but he didn't notice. He was too busy doing more flips in the air. A pack of floating string cheese bumped him next. He unwrapped it and took a big bite.

THIS was my crew? Neptune help me.

CHAPTER NINE
Two Telescopes and a Free-Floating Pup

Professor Cheetah," Ash said, "chart a course to our first stop. The Hubble Space Telescope."

"Hey, I'm the captain," I protested. "I decide where to go."

"Trust me, you'll want to see this." Ash grinned. Well, at least they weren't moping about Leo and the snot.

"Okay, fine," I said.

I took my spot in the chair by the control panel and put on my seat belt. Luckily, there were enough seats and space suits for when we got to Neptune, even though we had some stowaways. I guess Professor Cheetah had designed extras.

She pushed some buttons, and the rockets fired again. Soon, we were floating next to the giant space telescope.

"Wow," I said. "It's bigger than I thought. But isn't the Webb Telescope even bigger?"

"Yeah, it is," Ash said. "Did your mom tell you about Webb?"

I nodded. "It's a lot newer than Hubble, right? She showed me some really pretty pictures of nebulas and stars and stuff that came from Webb."

"Yeah, they're both really cool," Ash said. "But they're different. Hubble orbits around Earth, circling it every ninety-five minutes. But Webb doesn't spin around the Earth. Instead, it sticks beside Earth, and they both orbit the sun together."

"What do we use them for?" I asked.

"They both take pictures of faraway planets, stars, and galaxies. But Webb can see far away

39

stars more clearly than Hubble. It can even see the earliest galaxies and stars that formed in the universe. Isn't that cool?"

"Huh? I don't get it," I said. "How can it see something that happened a long time ago?"

"Because," Ash answered, "even though light travels really fast, the universe is so big that it takes a really long time to get to us. So the farther away we look, the farther into the past we're actually seeing."

"That's kind of confusing," I said. "You really understand all of that?"

Ash shrugged. "I did a lot of research for my science fair project. Some of the secrets of the universe are definitely cool and weird and a little hard to understand. But yes, Webb can look into the past. It can also take great pictures of Neptune. Your mom told me her lab work uses a lot of information coming from both Hubble and Webb—including the data that led to the Great Diamond Experiment."

"Well, that part is definitely cool," I admitted. "Can we get some of its pictures on our screen?"

Professor Cheetah pushed the buttons on the control panel, which made a bunch of beeping sounds. Fluff Monster growled at each one. Then came a long, slow beep. It upset Fluff Monster so much that she escaped from Abu's grip and hurled herself toward the computer.

"Oof!" I yelped. "Fluff Monster, don't mess with the controls!"

But she pushed a button with her nose anyway. The screen lit up with a picture—of a beautiful deep blue planet. Phew, she hadn't messed anything up.

"It's Neptune!" Ash said. "Clouds of methane gas give it the blue color."

"It's so pretty," I said, leaning closer.

Munch. Munch. Munch.
Abu had brought pakoras! Yum.

"Hey, let me have some of those," I said, trying to grab one from his tin.

"Hey!" Abu said, slapping my hand. "I thought you didn't want me to come."

I narrowed my eyes. "Well, I didn't."

"Then you don't get any pakoras," he said.

"Fine!" I yelled.

"Arf!" Fluff Monster barked.

Ash floated between us. "Come on, guys, we're all here now. Let's try to get along."

"Okay." I felt tears welling up in my eyes again, but I wasn't going to be the one to throw a tantrum. I was still the big sister.

CHAPTER TEN
The Problem with Air Gymnastics

Soon we'd reached the Webb Telescope, which Ash told us was a million miles from Earth.

"We already traveled a million miles?" I asked, peering out the window to get a better look.

"I guess so!" Ash said. "Cardboard box magic is really powerful!"

"But I thought you said Webb sticks next to Earth?"

Ash pointed to the flight path on the control panel. "Everything in the solar system is spread really far apart. So a million miles is really close when you're talking about objects in space."

It did look close on the flight path. A lot closer than Neptune, anyway.

I turned back to the window. Hubble had looked more like the telescope Mom had in my parents' bedroom—it was a cylinder with a mirror on the end. But Webb wasn't shaped like a cylinder. It had a flat stand, and its mirror stuck out like a chair on top of it. The chair part was made up of a bunch of hexagons.

"Webb can see farther away—and farther into the past—than Hubble because its mirror is so much bigger," Ash explained.

I liked listening to Ash talk about science because they loved it so much. They fit right in with the grown-ups in my family. I thought science was cool too, but I was always most excited about new adventures.

Seeing Hubble and Webb had also made Ash forget about Leo and the Snot Disaster. And maybe Abu and Fluff Monster would be good for once.

They were entertaining themselves with lots of air gymnastics. Fluff looked so cute trying to chase after floating kibble, even though her legs bicycling didn't really get her where she wanted to be.

Well, it was cute . . . right until she accidentally leapt onto the control panel again. And her paws pressed some more random buttons. The rockets roared to life, and suddenly the ship was flying fast! Professor Cheetah scrambled at the controls.

"Ack!" I grabbed on to my chair to steady myself. "We're still headed to Neptune, right?"

"Let me see . . ." Professor Cheetah peered at the screen, then shook her head. "Unfortunately, your canine friend changed our course. We were planning to use Jupiter as a gravity assist. Swinging around it would give us the speed and momentum we need to get to Neptune. But now we're going the wrong way. It takes a lot of fuel to steer the ship, and according to my calculations, we don't have enough to fix this mistake."

I looked at our fuel levels. "Wait a minute. I thought Imagination Fuel was limitless."

Professor Cheetah's tail wagged. "No, no, no. Once the cardboard box changed into a spaceship, our Imagination Fuel changed into regular fuel. And we've already burned through way too much."

Our school guidance counselor always told us to name our feelings. Well, I knew exactly what I was feeling just then: mad.

If Fluff Monster hadn't snuck on board, we wouldn't be in this mess!

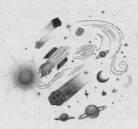

CHAPTER ELEVEN
Mission: Hunting for Kibble

Professor Cheetah was deep into her math equations, working on a solution to get us back on track. She was muttering a lot, so I didn't think it was going well. Meanwhile, Ash was just playing with Fluff Monster and Abu like we weren't going way off course.

Was I the only one who cared about diamonds?

"Maybe I can help," I said to Professor Cheetah. "Explain the problem to me again. Something about Jupiter?"

"Our plan was to use a Jupiter gravity assist to help us get to Neptune," she said. "*Voyager 2* launched in 1977 and—"

"It was the only spacecraft that ever passed near Neptune," Ash chimed in, finally paying attention to us.

Professor Cheetah's whiskers twitched at the interruption. "Yes, yes. It used the gravity of Jupiter to speed itself up and slingshot around the planet toward Saturn. Back then, the outer planets were lined up just right in their orbits so that *Voyager 2* was able to visit each of them. We're not that lucky. That special line up only happens about once every one hundred seventy-six years. But I did calculate this path we could take."

She pointed to a map of the solar system with a pink dotted line that spiraled out from Earth, swung around Jupiter, and then on to Neptune. The path around Jupiter looked like a roller-coaster loop, and it sounded fun to use it as a slingshot. Too bad we weren't on the path anymore.

Saturn and Uranus were in their orbits on the

other side of the sun, so they wouldn't help us get to Neptune either.

"Where are we now?" I asked.

"We're headed this way." Professor Cheetah drew a new orange dotted path that went into the asteroid belt, where lots of big rocks hung out. From there, the orange path continued out of the solar system.

Which would be pretty cool to explore, but even at cardboard box speed, we wouldn't be able to make it back in time to impress Nani and Nana with the space diamonds.

"Arf!" Fluff Monster barked.

Another bunch of floating kibble bits went past her. She tried to scramble toward it, but she didn't have anything to push off of to give her speed and momentum. Her ears perked up, the way they did when she had an idea. Instead of scrambling toward the kibble, she waited. She let herself float slowly away from the kibble, toward one of the walls. When she finally reached it, she pushed off of it to a second wall. Then she pushed off again, this time even more strongly, to get right in the path of the kibble.

She chomped it happily, very proud of herself. Which she should be. I couldn't believe how fast she'd picked up how to navigate in weightlessness! In fact, she'd also given me a brilliant idea.

CHAPTER TWELVE
Double Gravity Assist

Did you see what Fluff Monster did?" I asked. "She waited until her own momentum took her to the wall. Then she used two different walls to kick herself to the kibble."

"How does that help us?" Professor Cheetah looked at her map.

I pointed to a red planet. "If we wait, Mars will be in our path soon. Everything is moving at every second, remember?"

"I get it now!" Professor Cheetah grinned her

scary cheetah grin. "Good thinking. It could be like a wall for us—a second gravity assist!"

Ash nudged me. "Not bad for an eight-year-old."

I rolled my eyes. "Um . . . thanks. Except eight-year-olds are amazing."

Ash smiled. "I guess they are, little cuz."

Then they leapt on me, and we started air-wrestling. Fluff Monster barked excitedly, and Abu somersaulted toward us. We were a whirling dangerous mass. Mom would definitely have told us to calm down and be more careful.

"Ow!" I said as I banged into a wall.

"Oof!" Abu said as we banged again.

"Yikes!" Ash said as they pushed us away from the ceiling.

"Arf!" Fluff said.

"We're approaching Mars!" Professor Cheetah called, whiskers twitching as she laughed at our antics. "Hang tight!"

When the moment was right, we sped toward Mars using more of our precious fuel. As we got near the big red planet, its gravity pulled us into its orbit and spun us quickly around. Our ship then had the momentum to shoot off toward Jupiter.

The flight path for the gravity assist had looked like a roller-coaster loop, and it felt like one too!

As we sped through the asteroid belt, though, things calmed down. I was confused. There weren't any rocks hurtling dangerously toward us. Just stars and planets safely in the distance.

"Where are all the asteroids?" I asked. "I thought we'd have to dodge through them like in a video game."

"Remember how I said the Webb Telescope is a million miles from Earth? Space is really big," Ash said. "So even though there are a lot of asteroids in the belt, they're actually spread pretty far apart. You don't need to dodge through them."

"We have a clear path to Jupiter," Professor Cheetah said. "Smooth sailing the whole way."

"Oh," I said. That wasn't exactly adventure worthy. But at least we were getting closer to Neptune.

CHAPTER THIRTEEN
Pit Stop

The double slingshot brought us quickly to Neptune. Mom would say it was impossible, since it took *Voyager 2* twelve years. Even with the Imagination Fuel turned into boring regular fuel, I guess the cardboard box magic still had some uses. I spotted the arcs of Neptune's rings first.

"Cool!" Abu said, his nose pressed against the window.

"What're they made of?" I asked.

"Just dark space dust," Ash said. "See the

shinier parts? They're reflecting sunlight. The dark parts aren't."

"Arf!" Fluff Monster put her paws up on the window.

"Uh-oh!" said Abu. "When Fluffy puts her paws up, that means she needs to go potty."

Unfortunately, Abu was right.

"Oh great," I said. "Why does she always need to do her business when we're in the middle of something? We're so close to the diamonds! Plus, we just took her for a walk!"

"Maybe we can take her for a pit stop right there?" Ash said, pointing. "Is that Triton, Neptune's biggest moon?"

"Exactly right." Professor Cheetah steered the spaceship—using up more of our precious fuel to fire the thrusters.

I'd known that Fluff Monster was going to make everything revolve around her. From the moment I'd woken up, I'd been excited to go on an adventure. But first she'd eaten my ideas notebook. Then I had to take her for a walk. And now we had to go to Triton so Fluff Monster could go potty.

"Arf!" Fluff Monster said again.

Great Neptune! If we didn't take her out soon, she'd have an accident. And without any gravity to hold it in place, Fluff Monster's business would spread all over the spaceship.

"Okay, okay," I muttered. "Let's get this over with."

Professor Cheetah landed the ship on Triton's icy surface, and Fluff Monster ran out in her doggie space suit. We all had to wear the special suits that Professor Cheetah had designed, since Triton didn't have oxygen to breathe—and because of the extreme temperatures. The suits had a built-in radio communication system so we could talk to each other with our thick helmets on.

"Triton is one of the coldest places in the solar system, -391 degrees Fahrenheit!" Ash informed us through the radio. "Earth only has one moon, but this is just one of Neptune's. It has at least thirteen others, and scientists think there might still be more."

"Maybe we'll discover a new one," I said, squinting out into space. "I know exactly what we could call it: Sejal!"

Ash looked thoughtful. "That would make a pretty good name for a moon. Although Ash would be pretty good too."

"Maybe Sejal Ash?" I offered.

"I'll take it!" Ash grinned.

Fluff Monster wasn't interested, though. She tugged hard on the leash.

"Um, Professor Cheetah, how is Fluff Monster supposed to go potty in her suit?" I asked. "Do I have to take it off?"

"No! You can't do that in this cold," Professor Cheetah said. "But don't worry, the suit is designed to get rid of, um, the waste. You probably don't want me to go into the details."

Through her helmet, I could see her whiskers twitching with laughter. She was right. I probably didn't need to know the details.

"Okay, go potty!" I commanded Fluff.

She did her business (which worked somehow) and then she was ready to explore. With her tail wagging, she seemed like she was having a lot of fun sliding all over the sheets of methane ice. She tugged really hard on the leash again, and even though she was small, it was enough to make me slip. I fell down on my knees and accidentally let go of her. Fluff Monster scampered across the surface of Triton, which had little craters and grooves everywhere like the rind of a cantaloupe.

"See?" Abu shouted. "This time YOU let go of the leash!"

He had a point. But before I could answer, there was a loud KABOOM!

"What was that?" I shouted.

"An ice volcano!" Ash shouted. "We need to get back to the ship now!"

I tried to get up, but huge amounts of dust and gas burst out, knocking me back to the ground. Wind blew the dust everywhere so I couldn't see a thing.

"Sejal, Abu, are you okay?" Ash shouted.

"Yeah, I'm here," Abu said.

"Me too. Professor Cheetah?" I asked, trying to be calm. "How about you?"

"I don't like the smell of this place, but I'm fine."

"Fluff Monster?"

At first nothing but static came through. My heart squeezed with worry for my naughty but also sweet little perfect pup. Sure, she was constantly getting into trouble and chewing on my notebooks. But I loved her and didn't want anything bad to happen to her.

"Fluff?" I asked again.

Then I heard the absolute best sound in the solar system.

"Arf!"

Fluff Monster was still okay.

CHAPTER FOURTEEN
Abandon Ship

Four more ice volcanoes blew up with a ton of dust and gas as we raced back to the spaceship. Dear Triton, this was too much! We lifted off, using the last of our fuel. As we soared toward the big blue planet, I had no idea how we'd ever get back to Earth. At least everyone was safe on board. Silly puppies and all.

"How do you land on a planet made of liquid and gas?" I asked once we got going again.

"That's a good question," Ash said. "There is

no solid surface, no ground like there is on Earth. First, we'll enter the atmosphere, the cloud layer that surrounds the planet. As we move farther inward, there will be more pressure and heat around us. The gases will give way to Neptune's slushy liquid interior. We'll probably end up floating somewhere inside there. That's if we make it past the windstorms, of course."

A thrill went through me. The windstorms were exactly the kind of adventure I'd wanted to go on. And maybe having Abu and Fluff Monster around wasn't such a bad thing either, since Fluff's potty break had been pretty thrilling too.

All this danger would make the diamond souvenirs even more special.

"Keep your space suits on, and buckle up!" I called, helping Abu and Fluff Monster with their seatbelts.

"Here," Abu said, handing me a pakora. "I guess you can have one now."

"Thanks." I took off my helmet to munch it quickly—yum! And then put the helmet right back on. We needed to be ready for those wind-storms.

The ship rattled as we climbed into a foggy sea of clouds. Gravity at the outer edge of Neptune's atmosphere was not much different from that on Earth, and the ship fell toward Neptune's interior fast.

We heard a sound like a distant ocean wave.

"What is that?" I asked.

It sounded just a teeny bit scary, and it was getting steadily louder until it was a roar all around us.

"We're inside a storm stronger than any of Earth's hurricanes," Ash said.

Superfast winds pulled at our ship. The storm ripped the left thrusters off. Then the right thrusters. Then a piece of the spaceship's nose.

Screeching, ripping sounds came next—after our ship had already lost the parts. That was weird. Did I say I was a teensy bit scared before? Now I was really, really, *really* scared.

"These winds are supersonic—faster than the speed of sound!" Professor Cheetah explained, looking at the controls. "That's why the ripping sounds are delayed."

Wow. We were in a storm with winds faster than the speed of sound? So cool!

"Yeah, but what are we going to do about it?" Ash asked. "The ship's totally falling apart!"

I grinned. It was scary, but also pretty exciting.

"We need to abandon ship," I called. "Get ready!"

When I pressed the eject button, the seat belts unclicked. Then we were either flying or swimming or falling through gas and liquid. Actually, we were flying *and* swimming *and* falling, all at once. I switched on my space suit lights.

After all, we'd come all this way for a reason. It was time to hunt diamonds.

CHAPTER FIFTEEN
Diamond Rain: THE BEST THING EVER.

We fell and swam and fell some more. We were deep inside the ocean of Neptune's interior!

"What is all this slushy stuff?" I asked through the radio comm system. "It's not water. Or ice. I thought Neptune was called an ice giant?"

"It is," Ash said. "Even though it's actually very, very hot inside Neptune, scientists call it 'icy' because of the slushy hot dense mix of liquid and solid stuff found here: water, ammonia, and methane."

"Um, I think scientists should think of a better name, since icy and hot are opposites," I muttered.

"Agreed," Ash said.

"Suit check!" Professor Cheetah called. "Is everyone comfortable? I designed them to keep us cozy and safe. With my special engineering, they should be able to resist all the heat and pressure, which is good because otherwise we'd be melted and smooshed flat."

"Feeling fine," I said.

"Yep," Ash confirmed. "Good job, Professor Cheetah!"

"Fine, but I forgot my snacks," Abu whined.

"Arf! Arf! Arf!" Fluff said.

Thank Triton! The Sinha Squad was okay. Actually, that name had a nice ring to it. It really was fun to have everyone here for the adventure.

"Go Sinha Squad!" I yelled. "Let's get treasure hunting!"

THUMP!

Ouch. I landed on a huge, glittering rock. Wait a minute—what had Ash said about how big the diamonds on Neptune were? Could this really be . . . ?

It was. It really was.

"I'm standing on a giant diamond iceberg!" I yelled into the comm. "How is this possible?"

"Ooh, this is perfect practice for my science presentation!" Ash said, clearing their throat and putting on a very professional voice. "You see, the diamond rain has to do with its chemical structure."

"Huh?" I asked.

"Um, I'm trying to explain!" Ash said.

"Explain faster," I returned. There were more beautiful diamonds falling down around us. It was sort of like rain and sort of not, since we were already surrounded by slush.

"Okay, okay," Ash said. "Don't be so impatient. So you know that atoms are these tiny things that are too small to see and make up everything in our world?"

"Um, I'm in third grade!" I said. "Of course I know about atoms."

Ash rolled their eyes. "When two or more atoms attach together, they create a molecule. One really important molecule found on Neptune is methane, which has carbon atoms and hydrogen atoms. Here in the interior, there's lots of pressure—that means the feeling of being smooshed. And it's also super hot. The smooshy pressure and heat make the molecules change. The carbon atoms in the methane get squeezed out into a repeated pattern called a crystal structure. And that crystal pattern forms . . ."

"Diamonds!" Abu, Professor Cheetah, and I shouted together.

Ash grinned. "That's right. The diamonds are heavy and dense, so they fall through the other slushy liquids down to the core, like rain. When the diamonds hit other carbon atoms, they attach to each other. The diamonds get bigger and bigger until they make giant diamond bergs."

"Wow," I said.

"Yep! But at the core, it's even hotter, hot enough to melt part or maybe all of the diamond berg back into liquid carbon. Those carbon atoms will then float back up through the slushy interior and rejoin with some hydrogen atoms back into methane."

"So it's a cycle," I said. "Just like how it rains water on Earth. Water vapor makes clouds. When there's enough water, the cloud gets heavy and it rains. Then the water evaporates and turns back into clouds."

"Exactly!" Ash said. "When the smooshy pressure squeezes out the carbon atoms, the whole diamond rain cycle starts again."

"So cool," I said. "I still can't believe I'm standing on a diamond berg."

"Me either!" Professor Cheetah said. "We'll be rich!"

"Arf!" said Fluff Monster.

"Neat!" said Abu.

It was really raining diamonds all around us. It wasn't theoretical anymore. Luckily, our helmets were protecting our heads, or we'd get seriously bonked!

The diamond berg was too big to bring home, but I started catching the smaller diamonds falling like snowflakes around me. I tucked them safely into my handy sample collection bag. Nani and Nana would be blown away when we came home with real diamonds!

But as I filled my bag, I felt a weird sinking sensation. First slowly. Then faster and faster.

"Ahhhh!" I screamed as the diamond berg sank toward Neptune's rocky molten core. The soles of my space boots had melted a little, and that made them stick to the sinking diamond berg. I tried to swim up, but the berg was stuck to me and way too heavy.

In my hand, I held what we'd come for—the precious bag of diamonds. But with my melting boots and the diamond berg pulling me down, would I be able to make it home?

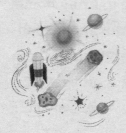

CHAPTER SIXTEEN
Boots on Fire

I rode the diamond iceberg like a snowboard down toward the molten rocky core of Neptune. Luckily, the space suit kept me safe even as it got hotter and hotter. That was good, but what was not so good was the diamond berg melting right at my feet. My space boots were getting way too hot.

OUCH.

Even with Professor Cheetah's magic touch, I was pretty sure the temperatures of the core would melt the space suit and me, too, if I didn't

change direction soon. But how was I supposed
to do that without any thrusters to take me up
toward the surface?

"Mayday! Mayday!" I yelled into the comm.
"Does anyone know how to get out of here?"

"I'm working on something!" Professor
Cheetah said.

"Work faster!" Abu said.

"Arf!" Fluff Monster agreed.

"Let me know if I can help," Ash added.

Professor Cheetah purred. Cheetahs actually do not ever roar, but they can purr, meow, or even chirp like a bird. And Professor Cheetah sometimes purred when she was annoyed. So I tried to be patient. It was kind of hard with my boots on fire, though.

Professor Cheetah didn't let me down. Soon, she and Ash came zooming toward me in the cardboard box, which looked a bit beat-up but didn't seem to have completely fallen apart in the windstorm. Cardboard boxes really are magical! Plus, it was flying with new rockets. I jumped into it just as the diamond berg at my feet melted into the thick liquid carbon layer that surrounded the core.

"We were out of fuel!" I said. "How'd you get more?"

"Neptune has its own internal heat source," Ash said. "In fact, it creates more heat than it gets from the sun."

Professor Cheetah grinned her big, toothy

cheetah grin. "And guess what? Heat can be changed into energy. So I invented a nifty converter that will take us all the way home."

"You're brilliant!" I said.

"I know," she returned. "But Ash helped."

Even though Professor Cheetah was a know-it-all show-off, it was really cool that she and Ash were able to work together. Of course, I sort of wished that I had also helped invent a way to convert Neptune's heat into energy. But sometimes a girl had to accept when her older cousin and stuffie had talents she didn't. (Even though I know plenty!)

Abu waved to us from a diamond berg up ahead. He had Fluff Monster next to him—with the leash attached to her space harness. I couldn't believe how glad I was to see my brother and that silly pup.

"You found Fluff Monster!" I said.

"She really wanted to eat all the diamonds," Abu said. "She thinks they're kibble. I'm glad I caught her before she wiggled out of her helmet."

"You're really good with her," I admitted.

"Thanks, Didi."

Uh-oh. Didi meant big sis. He only called me that when he wanted something.

"Since I'm so responsible," he said with a hopeful look, "you'll let me hold the leash next time we take her for a walk, right?"

"Um . . ." I wanted to say yes, but I was still a little worried. "Let's talk about that when we get home."

Professor Cheetah pulled the cardboard box alongside Abu. But Abu was definitely wearing his stubborn face. The one he usually got right before he had a huge tantrum. Oh no.

I tried bribing him. "If you jump in, you can have all the string cheese you want as soon as you get home. I promise!"

But Abu picked up Fluff Monster and held her tightly. "I'm not getting in unless you promise to let me hold her leash!"

"We don't have time for this!" I waved at him to jump in. "We need to get home!"

"Promise!" yelled Abu.

Good geysers! Abu had kept Fluff Monster safe here on Neptune, so he was sort of responsible. For a five-year-old. Besides, if he didn't get in before our fuel ran out, we'd never get back to Earth either way.

"Sometimes you have to trust," Ash said.

That was the part of being a big sister that was hard for me. But Ash had been patient with me when I'd almost cried about not getting the alone time with them that I'd wanted. In fact, Ash was always patient with me. They didn't treat me like a little kid. So maybe I had to stop treating Abu like one. Maybe I could reason with him.

"Okay, okay!" I finally said. "You can hold the leash—if you stop throwing tantrums when you don't get your way. Deal?"

Abu didn't stop to think. "Yesssss!!!"

He jumped into the cardboard box with Fluff Monster.

"Arf!" said Fluff Monster.

With the entire crew in the cardboard box,

I pressed the green triangle button. The box changed back into a spaceship. Abu had better keep his part of the deal—but I'd worry about that when we made it back to Earth.

CHAPTER SEVENTEEN
The "Monster" in Fluff Monster, Part Two

We rocketed up the interior of Neptune. Well, for a minute. Then we slowed way down. Not cool, rocket ship. Not cool.

"What's happening?" I asked. "Will we be able to exit Neptune's atmosphere?"

Outside the ship's window, the liquid interior of Neptune was giving way to blue methane clouds and fog. Wind was blowing fiercely again, and the spaceship rattled. Storms had already broken parts of the ship once, and I didn't want to go through that again. I'd had enough adventures. Now I just wanted to go home.

"I don't know why we're not going faster!" Professor Cheetah said. "I calculated the weight of everyone in the crew, including Fluff Monster, but for some reason we're not getting the lift we need."

Oof! I started jamming all the buttons. Something had to work!

"That's not going to help," Professor Cheetah said unhelpfully.

"Arf!" barked Fluff Monster as she sniffed my sample bag, which was attached to the belt of my space suit.

"Did you find some yummy treats?" Abu said.

"It's not a treat bag," I explained. "I collected some diamond—"

But before I could finish, Fluff Monster grabbed the bag between her teeth and tugged hard, managing to rip the bag's ties and get it free. Then Fluff darted between my legs and ran away. Since we were still inside Neptune's atmosphere, its gravity was still strong enough to keep us on the floor. And Fluff Monster can be annoyingly fast, especially when I'm chasing her.

"Help me, Abu!" I said. "She listens to you."

"Fluff Monster, COME!" Abu called.

Oh, yeah, we'd learned the special doggie command in Fluff Monster's puppy training class. You had to say the exact right word and say it exactly the same way every time. Abu was better than me at remembering those things. Fluff Monster came right to him. She dropped the bag of diamonds at his feet.

"Good girl!" Abu bent to pick it up.

But Fluff Monster was too quick for him. She snatched the bag and darted away again.

"COME!" Abu repeated, but this time Fluff Monster ignored him.

"How is she even lifting up all those diamonds?" Ash asked, chasing after the naughty pup. "They're really heavy."

"Heavy?" Professor Cheetah's whiskers twitched. "Wait, let me see those."

She chased after Fluff Monster too. Cheetahs are the fastest land animals on Earth, so there was no way that Fluff could outrun her. But Fluff jumped onto the control panel just a second before Professor Cheetah's pounce.

"No, don't!" I yelled.

But it was too late. Fluff Monster pressed the green triangle button.

The ship suddenly converted back into a cardboard box. She leaned over the side and yapped with delight. She always loved the wind in her face when she stuck her head out of the car window.

But when she yapped, she dropped the bag of diamonds overboard. I desperately reached out, trying to catch it, but it was no use. The diamonds were gone.

CHAPTER EIGHTEEN
Saved by a Silly Pup

Professor Cheetah pressed the green triangle button again. The cardboard box switched back into a spaceship. It picked up speed and rocketed past Neptune's atmosphere. Then we passed the planet's fourteen known moons. We sped out of the rings made of ice and dust.

I hung my head. My stomach squeezed. How could I go home without the diamonds? Without them, it would be like we'd never even left Earth at all. So much for getting Nani and Nana the best souvenir ever.

Fluff Monster bounced and floated over to me and licked me in the face.

"I love you, Fluff," I said sadly, "but why did you do that?"

"She saved us," Professor Cheetah said. "The diamonds were too heavy. I forgot to include them in my calculations for liftoff."

"So you're saying she wasn't just being naughty?" I asked.

Professor Cheetah's whiskers twitched. "I wouldn't go that far."

"Maybe she just wanted to dig a hole and bury them to save for later," Ash said. "Of course, she can't tell us, since she only speaks puppy."

"Arf!" Fluff Monster said.

Even though I was sad to leave the diamonds, I knew it was good we'd all made it off Neptune and were headed home. Plus, I remembered how worried I'd felt when I thought Fluff had gotten lost in the ice volcano on Triton. As naughty as she was, she was like my baby sister. But even for-giving her didn't take my sadness away.

I'm not proud of it, but I may have moped all the way home. Soon we landed back in the basement. Our rocket ship became an ordinary cardboard box.

"Ooh, it smells like dinner is ready," Ash said. "Your dad is the best cook!"

"I'm soooo hungry!" Abu disappeared up the stairs.

"Save me some good bites!" Professor Chee-tah's whiskers twitched.

I didn't say anything. Instead, I started doing something I almost never did unless my parents made me—clean up. After all, I was a big sister, and that's what big sisters did. Abu had left an empty string cheese wrapper on the floor, so I threw it away. Then I folded the cardboard box and put it in the closet.

"Hey, are you okay?" Ash asked. "You're . . . cleaning. On purpose. Without being told."

I just shrugged and started putting markers back into their box.

"Now I know something is wrong." Ash helped me pick up.

I sighed. "Well, our mission was a failure. We have no diamonds."

They nodded. "True. But you know what? I had fun escaping Earth with you—even if it was only for a little while."

"But we didn't get to hang just the two of us. Fluff Monster and Abu always hog all the attention."

Ash giggled. "Yeah, sometimes they do. That's part of the fun. But when I think of this trip, I'll definitely remember that *you* were the captain." They put a hand on my shoulder. "Sejal, you've got some of the most powerful Imagination Fuel there is. You even helped me forget all about the Snot Disaster! And now that I've had some time away, I'm over it. Everyone has snot. Who cares?"

I hugged them. "Thanks, Ash. I'm glad you're feeling better about snot."

They squeezed me back, and that was better than diamonds.

CHAPTER NINETEEN
Unexpected Visitor

Dad had made one of my favorite foods for dinner. Pani poori—round fried balls of dough that we filled with chutneys, sauces, chickpeas, and other yummy seasoned food. They were small enough that I could stuff the whole poori into my mouth. The sauces spilled out when I crunched, and it was amazing.

"It's just as good as the street food in India," Nani said.

"Oh, you're exaggerating," Dad said.

"No, really," Nana insisted. "I think Sameer would approve. He runs our favorite pani poori cart in Kolkata."

I could tell that Dad was happy with all the compliments. Nani and Nana told us more about all the yummy food they'd had in India, places they'd visited, and relatives I usually only saw on video calls.

Abu gobbled up his pani poories so fast, they were gone in just a few minutes. Then he stared at his empty plate. Uh-oh. Was this going to be like the Disappearing String Cheese Tantrum of this morning? I waved for his attention, and then gave him my best big-sister-warning look to remind him of his promise. It was kind of like the squinty look mom got right before assigning me extra homework.

It worked. He took a deep breath. "Can I have more, please?"

"Of course!" Dad said. "Thanks for asking politely."

As Dad plopped more poories on Abu's plate, the doorbell rang.

"Hmm, I wonder who that is," Mom mused, getting up to check.

We heard voices along with Fluff's barking as my mom opened the door. It sounded like a kid had come, but I wasn't sure who. Ash suddenly looked very alert, though.

I understood why when a few moments later, Leo came to the dining table.

"Hey," he said to Ash.

"Hey," said Ash.

They both just kind of stared at each other. Ash was getting that funny look on their face, the same one they'd had at the park. Were they worried that Leo would make fun of them? They'd said they were over the Snot Disaster. Plus, they'd acted strangely around him at the park even before the sneezing attack.

"Well, hello, young man," Nana boomed. "Sit down and join us!"

Dad grabbed an extra plate for Leo, and Nani showed him how to poke a hole in the pani poori and then stuff it with delicious fillings.

"This is really good!" Leo said. "Indian food is the best."

Everyone in my family loved to hear that—especially since Leo didn't complain about it being too spicy, either. He did take a big gulp of water, though.

Then he turned to Ash. "Did you finish your science report?"

"Not yet, but I did do some field investigation!" Ash said. Their voice sounded a little funny too. What was it about Leo?

"Oh, did you go to your aunt's lab?" Leo asked.

Ash messed around with the food on their plate, not looking at him. "Um. Not exactly. Sejal and I . . ."

They didn't finish their sentence, just stared glumly at their food.

Oh no! Even after our trip, were they getting back into a funk? Maybe getting them to talk about science would help.

"We went to Neptune!" I burst out. "Do you want to see our spaceship after we eat?"

93

"Um, yeah!" Leo smiled. "That sounds awesome."

"I'd like to see it too," Nana said. "We've been talking so much about our trip to India, but now it's your turn. Tell us all about this adventure you had!"

Nani nodded in agreement.

I gulped. "Well, I wanted to get a souvenir for you both, but . . . we lost it."

"But we had a great time and learned a lot, right?" Ash said, suddenly excited again.

I nodded. I still didn't get why they acted so funny and shy around Leo, but at least talking about Neptune still made them happy.

CHAPTER TWENTY
A Different Kind of Souvenir

After we ate our fill, the whole family and Leo went down to the basement. I pulled the cardboard box out of the closet and unfolded it. To my surprise, Professor Cheetah was smooshed inside! How did that happen?

"Are you okay?" I asked, pulling her out.

She didn't answer. She was in one of her quiet moods, I guessed. Maybe she'd been working on fixing things up for our next trip.

"What a cool spaceship," Leo said, climbing into the cardboard box.

Nani, Nana, my parents, and Leo started asking us a ton of questions about our trip. Ash, Abu, and I told them all about the Hubble and Webb Space Telescopes, gravity assists, Triton's ice volcanoes, and how Professor Cheetah converted Neptune's heat into energy. And of course—the diamond rain.

I closed my eyes, remembering how amazing it had been to stand on that diamond berg with

glittering diamonds falling all around me like snow. "I put some in our sample bag to bring back as a souvenir, but Fluff Monster threw it overboard."

"She saved us," Ash reminded me. "The diamonds were too heavy for us to break out of Neptune's gravity pull."

"That's true," I said, scratching Fluff behind the ears. "Even though she probably didn't know she was saving us."

"Yes she did," Abu said. "She's really smart."

I sighed, sitting back down on the carpet. "But I really wanted the diamonds to give Nani and Nana as a souvenir. Since you brought us all those gifts from India."

Nana patted my shoulder kindly. "Sejal my dear, don't you see? Your story is your souvenir! All those details you told us were really something!"

"Really?" I asked. "Wouldn't you rather have a gift?"

Nana chuckled. "I think this was perfect."

"Wonderful," Nani added.

"I'm impressed by all the science in your story," Mom said. "Ash, you really learned your stuff."

"That gives me an idea!" Leo said. "I bet you could totally win the science fair if you bring your cousin and the spaceship and explain the science while telling an adventure story."

Ash looked surprised. "You think so?"

"Well, you might have some competition," Leo said. "I mean, I didn't get your snot, but I did get my little brother's. So I'm definitely gonna win something. How can boogers lose?"

Ash laughed. And then the two of them started talking about school and science and friends, and the Great Snot Disaster was totally forgotten. Ash's voice still sounded a little bit weirder than normal, though. Suddenly, I wondered if Ash had a crush?

Not that I knew much about crushes. I'd heard about some fifth graders getting them before, but I didn't really understand why. But Ash would tell me if they had one, wouldn't they?

CHAPTER TWENTY-ONE
A Sparkly Surprise

Maybe Nani and Nana were right. Who needs a souvenir when you have the best story to tell?

As Ash and Leo chatted, I rubbed Fluff Monster's soft furry back. She licked me—and then darted back into the cardboard spaceship, sniffing around inside. A moment later, she hopped right up to me. She was chewing on something. She was basically always chewing on something she wasn't supposed to.

"Do you have something in your mouth?" I asked.

Fluff Monster just tilted her head, waiting for a treat.

I grabbed a biscuit from the jar upstairs.

"Drop it," I said firmly but gently—just like Abu would. I couldn't believe I'd learned something from a five-year-old. I also offered the biscuit as an exchange.

Fluff Monster dropped the object in her mouth. It was covered in slobber and very dirty.

"What is it?" Nana's forehead crinkled.

My heart sped up. Could it be what I thought it was? I picked it up and took it to the bathroom sink, where I washed off the gunk all over it. When I came back, I felt like my smile was as bright as the sun.

"It's a diamond from Neptune!" I said, showing them the big sparkly stone. I couldn't believe it. I finally had my very own fancy souvenir. "For you, Nani and Nana."

I felt so proud when I handed it over.

"Arf!" said Fluff, butting her head against my leg.

"Okay, you get some credit too." I scratched her behind the ears. "Good girl, Fluff. You're a very, very good girl."

Author's Note

A lot of things about Neptune are still a mystery to us. Because it's so far away, none of our astronauts have ever been there. However, in 1989, an unmanned spacecraft from NASA called *Voyager* 2 flew within three thousand miles of Neptune. It took a lot of pictures and sent data back to Earth about the farthest planet in our solar system. Since then, we've gathered more data about Neptune from giant telescopes like the Hubble and Webb Space Telescopes.

So does it really rain diamonds on Neptune? Scientists think it's a possibility because of the chemical composition, heat, and pressure of the planet's interior. They've conducted experiments in laboratories to try to re-create those conditions. High-powered lasers can simulate the heat and pressure of Neptune and Uranus. And, yes, those experiments have resulted in the formation of tiny diamonds. This evidence suggests that diamond precipitation really does occur in the interior of those two farthest ice giant planets. But even if we could travel to Neptune in a reasonable amount of time, astronauts would also need a really amazing space suit to ever see the diamond rain because of the incredible heat and pressure they'd face! For now, how diamond rain would look will have to remain in our imaginations.

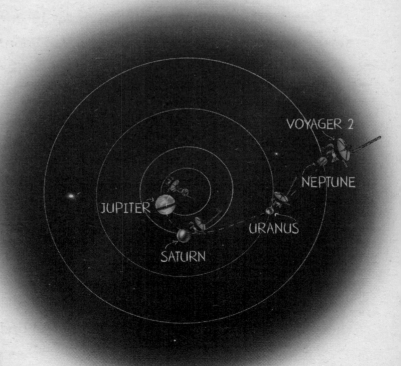

 Acknowledgments

As Sejal rockets into her third book, I'm so grateful for the brightly shining stars on my team: my agent Penny Moore, my editor Alyson Heller, and my illustrator Abira Das. Kristin Gilson, Valerie Garfield, Anna Jarzab, Olivia Ritchie, Heather Palisi, Amelia Jenkins, Anna Elling, Bezawit Yohannes, and the rest of the teams at Aladdin and Aevitas Creative Management: you're out of this world!

I still look back fondly on the days of my pre-pandemic in-person critique group, where I shared my earliest draft of a chapter book starring a girl named Sejal who wanted to check out the diamond rain on Neptune. Thanks so much Paul Decker, Zoe Fisher, and the rest of those brilliant writers for dreaming bookish dreams with me.

Mom and Dad, you've always helped me seek my path among the stars. Thank you.

This planet wouldn't be any fun without my

orbit buddies: my husband, kiddo, and loyal doggo. I'm so glad to rotate around the sun with all of you by my side.

Shout out to the constellation of parents, teachers, librarians, booksellers, and caregivers who seek out diverse reading for kids! Your guiding light is invaluable. And for the kid readers: Don't forget the Imagination Fuel!

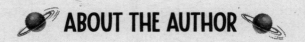 **ABOUT THE AUTHOR**

MAYA PRASAD is a South Asian American author, a Caltech graduate, and a former software engineer. She currently resides in the Pacific Northwest, where she enjoys hiking, kayaking, and writing stories with joyful representation for kids and teens.

The Sejal Sinha chapter book series was inspired by her own kiddo, who also has a favorite cheetah stuffie, an active imagination, and a trusty cardboard box. Visit her website MayaPrasad.com or find her on Instagram or TikTok @msmayaprasad.

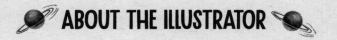

ABOUT THE ILLUSTRATOR

ABIRA DAS was born in India. As a child her biggest influences were watching her father drawing and painting and her love of Disney animation movies. Throughout the year you will find her sipping tea, bookworming, listening to music, intensely doodling while having telephonic conversations, traveling the world, expanding her collection of soft toys and action figures, binge watching anything she can, and enhancing her world of creativity.

READ& LEARN

with *simon* kids

Keep your child reading, learning,
and having fun with Simon Kids!

A one-stop shop where you can
**find downloadable resources, watch interactive author
videos, browse books by reading level, and more!**

**Visit us at
SimonandSchusterPublishing.com/ReadandLearn/**

And follow us @SimonKids

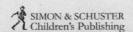
SIMON & SCHUSTER
Children's Publishing

Looking for another great book?
Find it
IN THE MIDDLE.

Fun, fantastic books for kids
in the in-be**TWEEN** age.

IntheMiddleBooks.com

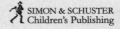 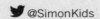

Don't miss the
Mindy Kim
series!

Join **Sejal Sinha** as she uses science and the power of imagination to go on adventures!